...making the meadow flowers sparkle and the green grass glisten.

T0370990

3

The fairies have invited their friends to a housewarming party...

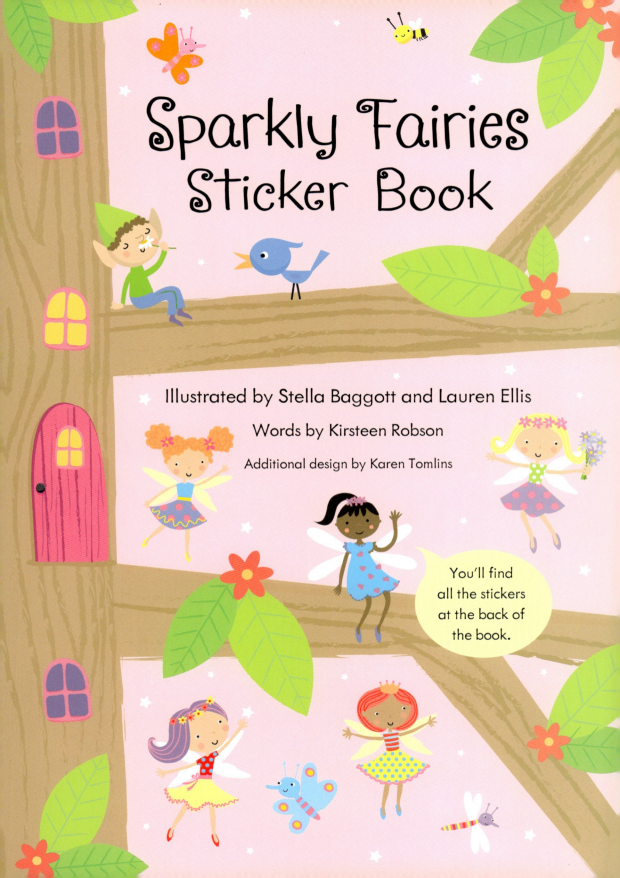

Sparkly Fairies
Sticker Book

Illustrated by Stella Baggott and Lauren Ellis

Words by Kirsteen Robson

Additional design by Karen Tomlins

You'll find all the stickers at the back of the book.

Early every summer morning the dew fairies sprinkle their diamond drops...

...to celebrate their new toadstool homes.

It's harvest time and fairy folk are gathering the ripe fruits.

Smooth acorns and rosy apples will

make tasty treats for dark winter days.

Fairies like to splash in the sparkling stream...

...while dazzling dragonflies dart around them.

8

The royal palace is fizzing with excitement...

...as everyone prepares for a magical masked ball.

Fairies stroke their glittering harps

and the dancers twirl to their tunes...

...while helpful elves carry in cakes and berrydew.

Flitting fairies and flickering fireflies
love to fly together in the silvery starlight.

Pages 2-3

Help the fairies sprinkle everything with dew.

Pages 4-5

Stick on a swarm of smiling visitors.

Pages 6-7

Show some busy elves and fairies.

Pages 8-9

Add fairies, flowers and a frog.

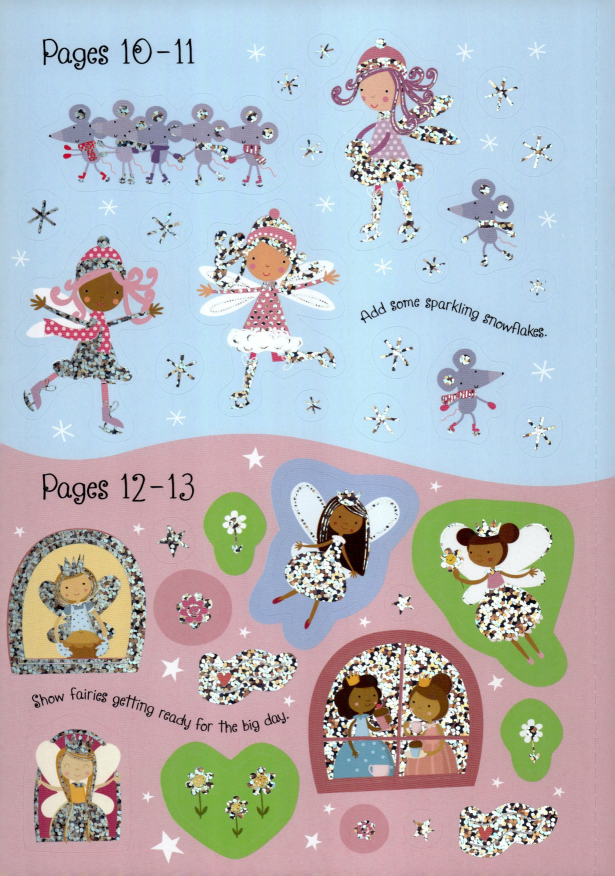

Pages 10-11

Add some sparkling snowflakes.

Pages 12-13

Show fairies getting ready for the big day.

Pages 14-15

Fill the ballroom with glamorous guests.

Page 16

Stick twinkling stars in the sky.

Pages 2-3

Fill the field with flowers.

Pages 4-5

Add some butterflies and bees.

Pages 6-7

Stick on more workers and animals.

Pages 8-9

Show some fairies having fun.

Pages 10-11

Arrange some skaters on the ice.

Pages 12-13

Fill the garden with flowers.

Pages 14-15

Scatter hearts everywhere!

Page 16

Add fairies and fireflies to finish the picture.